Shaun the Sheep

The

FARMER'S LLAMAS

FOR SALE

WITHDRAWN

FROM STOCK

First published 2015 by Walker Entertainment

An imprint of Walker Books Ltd

87 Vauxhall Walk, London SE11 5HJ

2 4 6 8 10 9 7 5 3 1

This book was typeset in ITC Cheltenham.

Printed and bound in Great Britain by Clays.

British Library Cataloguing in Publication Data: a catalogue record for this book is available from the British Library

ISBN 978-1-4063-6350-0

www.walker.co.uk

Shaun the Sheep™
The
FARMER'S LLAMAS

Martin Howard

WALKER
ENTERTAINMENT

CHAPTER ONE

SHAUN THE SHEEP SNIFFED the air. Somewhere close by, someone was baking. With little Timmy at his side, he peered into the kitchen window.

Inside, the Farmer and his trusty sheepdog, Bitzer, were both wearing frilly, blue aprons and matching chef's hats. The Farmer tossed a couple of eggs across the kitchen to Bitzer, who was whipping up a

 5

bowl of cake mixture. He added a few drops of green food colouring to some icing, then spooned it out and flattened it with a rolling pin while the chuckling Farmer took a tray of piping-hot biscuits shaped like sheep heads out of the oven.

Shaun stared, wide-eyed, at a huge cake. It was loaded with cream and had been decorated to look like a cakey version of Mossy Bottom Farm. For the finishing touch, the Farmer piped snowy white cream swirls onto the top layer while Bitzer popped the biscuit sheep heads into place. Hey presto: yummy sheep! Bitzer and the Farmer stepped back to consider their handiwork. The cake was a *masterpiece*. High-fiving each other, they hurried out of the kitchen.

Shaun's tummy rumbled. He looked at Timmy. Timmy looked back. They grinned at each other. A plan was forming in Shaun's mind: a plan that might well get him into lots of trouble, and have all kinds of unintended consequences. It was *exactly* his kind of plan.

A few seconds later, the cat flap in the front door squeaked and swung in as Shaun squeezed through. With a quiet snigger, Shaun checked the coast was clear, then tip-hoofed down the hall.

In his bedroom upstairs, the Farmer adjusted his bow tie. Bitzer brushed specks of dandruff from the Farmer's shoulders, then, job done, he stood back and adjusted his own bow tie while the Farmer turned this way and that, admiring himself.

Shaun crept along the hallway below. Stopping by the kitchen door, he peered in. The coast was clear. Eyes fixed on the cake, he sneaked round the kitchen table and lifted the baking masterpiece while Timmy opened the window, eagerly holding out his hooves.

Suddenly, they heard footsteps on the stairs and the Farmer's whistle. Shaun dropped the cake back onto the table and fled. Timmy dived into a flower bed.

Shaun scrambled for the hallway. The footsteps were louder now. Desperately, he looked around for a hiding place. There was nowhere, except the Farmer's coat hanging from its peg by the door.

With Bitzer close behind, the Farmer

stomped into the kitchen. Holding on to the inside of the coat, Shaun peeked out while Bitzer put the Mossy Bottom Farm cake into a box. Still whistling, the Farmer rubbed his hands together happily and stomped back to·the hallway, where he grabbed his coat and shrugged it on.

Hearing a strangely bleat-like sound, Bitzer looked up and down the hallway. What was that?

Struggling with his coat, the Farmer ignored the sheepdog. "Gah," he mumbled to himself. The zip wouldn't close. The coat was too tight. Shaking his head and glancing back at Bitzer, he patted his tummy in embarrassment. Perhaps it was time to go on a diet.

Bitzer glanced up and frowned, sorrow filling his heart. It looked like the Farmer, in his old age, was developing a hunch back.

Leaving his coat open, the Farmer bustled out of the front door and climbed into the car. Bitzer scrambled into the passenger seat and carefully positioned the precious cake box on his knees. Meanwhile, the Farmer snapped his seat belt into place and leaned back in his seat.

BEEAGHHHH!

The two of them looked at each other, then shrugged. That funny sound was probably just the squeaky old car making squeaky old car noises. With a cough and a roar, the engine rumbled into life. The Farmer steered out through the open gate and turned towards Mossy Bottom Village.

As he leaned back in his seat, another faint squeal came from the hunch in his coat. The Farmer grunted and squirmed. For some reason, he could not get comfy.

Timmy watched as the car roared past. He looked through the window into the kitchen, where the cake had been, and then round at the farm. Where was Shaun?

CHAPTER TWO

BITZER'S HEAD HUNG out of the window, his tongue flapping in the wind, while the car bumped and rattled along narrow roads edged with trees and fields. With a squeal of brakes, the Farmer swung the wheel. The car skidded into a field full of farm trucks and trailers. Beyond the car park, people nibbled ice lollies and wandered between stripy tents where prize vegetables and pedigree chickens were on display.

Eagerly, the Farmer scrambled out of the car—and yelped as he felt something squirm down the back of his coat. Then it was gone! Confused, he looked down. The coat seemed much looser now.

He shook his head. There was no time to puzzle over the mystery of the strange coat. With a whistle to Bitzer, he strode off, and the sheepdog trailed behind, staggering under the weight of the huge cake.

Shaun slipped under the car. Being squashed between the Farmer's back and the car seat had left him feeling like the filling in a sheep sandwich. Popping his ears back into their normal place, he gazed around. Close by, a man was selling buckets of fresh manure and yelling, "etcharuvverymanooooer. Honlytenpenshabukkit!" Next to him was a stall selling the latest in sheepdog whistle technology, which was exactly the same as old sheepdog whistle technology. A crowd of sheepdogs clustered round, panting in their eagerness to catch a glimpse of the new range of whistles, all of which looked identical to the old ones.

The Farmer and Bitzer walked to a large tent. By the opening was a wooden cut-out sign that showed a lady with a rolling pin, a chef's hat and a large cake with a cherry on top. The Farmer stopped and chuckled. His cake was sure to win first prize in the annual Mossy Bottom Cake-a-thon!

A moment later, his chuckle turned into a grunt as Bitzer bumped into his back. Turning, he scowled. "Whayahputeemach?" he grumbled at the sheepdog, then turned back again and hit his head on the wooden cake-lady's rolling pin. A bald man wearing red braces pointed and laughed. Still grumbling, the Farmer stomped into the cake tent.

Immediately, he brightened. This was more like it! The tent was packed with cakes, good and bad. An old lady was making what looked like a house of cards out of wafers. She would be no competition, the Farmer thought to himself. Some of the other cakes were much better, but he was still confident that his farm-cake would win. He adjusted his bow tie, then Bitzer's, and stood behind his masterpiece to wait for the judges.

Outside, Shaun shook his head and yawned. A country fair: *boring*. Ears twitching, he frowned. Over the squeak of the carousel and the shouts of the manure man, he heard a melodious sound, like the wind softly whistling through trees.

Turning, he saw a short man in a little black hat and a bright, multicoloured poncho walking through the crowd. In his hands, he held a set of wooden pipes into which he was blowing. The hypnotizing music wafted through the fairground. Three calm animals followed behind the man, led along by ropes.

Shaun stared. Apart from the teeth – Shaun was surprised they managed to get so many teeth into their mouths – the creatures looked like very tall sheep with long necks. Llamas! Shaun blinked. He'd never seen real-life llamas before.

The leader, whose name was Hector, was white with a brown tail. Behind him was a strong-looking llama named Raul, whose eyes were completely covered by dark-brown dreadlocks. Bringing up the rear was a white and caramel-coloured llama named Fernando, who was wearing patterned ankle warmers and a matching hat.

The music stopped abruptly. The piper had tripped over a tent peg and dropped the pipes! With a squeal, the man scrabbled through the grass for them.

Shaun hardly noticed. His attention was fixed on the llamas. As soon as the music had stopped, they had shaken their heads. The hypnotized look dropped from their eyes. Their faces changed. Peaceful calm disappeared, to be replaced by grins of wicked mischief.

The three llamas looked at one another, then turned and galloped across the grass, shouldering people aside as they headed straight for the cake tent. Behind them, the Peruvian piper was dragged through the fairground, hanging on to their lead ropes, squealing and shouting at the llamas to stop.

Ignoring him, they raced through the open flap of the tent. Shaun, hearing screams through the canvas walls, crept up to the tent and lifted the canvas to peer inside.

He was treated to a scene of chaos. Humans ran in circles, waving their arms in panic and trying to shoo the llamas away. Snorting with laughter, the llamas went into cake frenzy. They easily sidestepped the bake-off contestants as they knocked tables over, sending cakes flying and gobbling everything in sight.

Shaun's mouth dropped open in admiration. The llamas feasted on Victoria sponges and scones and iced buns and cream cakes decorated with strawberries. Hector, having put his head through a three-tiered fruitcake, noticed Shaun standing by. With a wink, the llama nudged a cupcake in Shaun's direction, then disappeared back into the screaming crowd, dragging the Peruvian piper along the length of a loaded table.

Shaun grinned as he munched his cupcake and watched icing fly. In the middle of it all, Bitzer whuffed, paws up, warding the llamas away from the Farmer's magnificent cake. The Farmer ducked as they charged past. At the last moment, Bitzer snatched the cake out of their way and breathed a sigh of relief.

At that moment, the Farmer stood up . . .

And put his head straight through the cake.

Once again, the bald man with red braces pointed and choked with laughter. Shaun, too, chuckled to himself. The llamas were amazing!

Within a few minutes, every cake had become an unrecognizable, soggy mess trampled into the floor or dripping down the canvas walls. Contestants wailed among overturned tables and chairs. Full of cake, and still dragging the pipe player on the end of their ropes, the llamas rushed for the exit. Struggling, the Peruvian yelped as he was dragged across the grass and made a desperate grab for his pipes as he was pulled past them.

A second later, the sound of pan pipes drifted across the field once more. The llamas stopped and fell into a neat line. Shaun blinked. The music turned them into completely different animals! Obediently, they followed the Peruvian piper as he headed for another tent. Fascinated, Shaun trotted after them.

Back in the cake tent, Bitzer picked up the Farmer's glasses and wiped cake from them, then peered through the smeared lenses to test them out. He glimpsed a familiar tail disappearing from the tent. *Shaun!*

Somehow Shaun had managed to get to the country fair. No wonder things had started going wrong! With a growl, Bitzer set off to find him.

Dazed, and still cleaning cake out of his ear, the Farmer wandered after him a few moments later.

Trailing after the pan-pipe music, Shaun watched the piper lead his llamas into another tent. Carefully, the small man shut them into a pen next to a podium where an auctioneer stood. People watched, nodding along to the haunting music and tapping their feet.

With a loud **CRACK,** the auctioneer brought his hammer down and shushed the piper. Reluctantly, he stopped playing.

Shaun watched as the llamas shook their heads once again. Suddenly, their eyes gleamed. Leaning over the bars of the pen, Fernando stretched out his long neck and tore a mouth-shaped hole in a magazine a man was reading. Raul snapped at the flowers in a lady's hat and chewed happily. Hector snatched the auctioneer's hammer. While the auctioneer tried to tug it back, Fernando tried to steal the flower from Raul's mouth. The petals tickled his nose. **_AHH . . . AHHH . . . ATCHOOO . . ._** The llama sneeze blew the auctioneer's wig into the crowd, where it landed on a baby's head.

Shaun snickered. The llamas were _awesome_. The ultimate pranksters!

Behind him, Bitzer pushed through the crowd. He was close. He could feel it! Wherever there was trouble, a Mossy Bottom sheep was sure to be involved.

By the entrance, the Farmer pushed aside the tent flaps and blinked around at the crowd. What was going on here? And where was Bitzer? Spotting Bitzer's hat, he whistled, loudly.

It was a whistle that Shaun recognized instantly. If the Farmer was here, then Bitzer would be close by. Quickly, he dived into the crowd of legs around him.

At the same moment, the auctioneer – who had recovered his wig – rapped his hammer to start the auction. Who wanted to buy the llamas? Were there any bids?

He waited a second.

Any bids at all?

People shook their heads.

By now, the Peruvian piper was sweating. As his three llamas carried on making stupid faces, sneezing and kicking at their pen, he prayed that someone – *anyone* – would buy them.

But no one was interested.

Ignoring the auctioneer, the Farmer waved to Bitzer.

On the podium, the auctioneer called out. He had his first bid from the balding man in the bow tie and glasses.

Bitzer waved back at the Farmer.

Again, the auctioneer shouted. A second bid!

The Farmer flapped a hand at the sheepdog, signalling him to come.

 25

Bitzer whuffed. At the podium, the auctioneer pointed at him with his hammer, shouted out a higher price and looked at the Farmer. Did he want to raise the price again?

Jerking his thumb over his shoulder, the Farmer signalled the sheepdog to meet him outside. Happily, the auctioneer raised the price again. At his side, the Peruvian couldn't believe his good fortune.

With a gulp, Bitzer finally realized what was going on. The auctioneer thought their waves were bids! The sheepdog leapt across the tent and grabbed the Farmer's arms before he could make another bid.

Shaun bleated in excitement. The Farmer was about to buy the llamas!

The auctioneer looked around for any last bids. In the crowd, a fly buzzed round the head of the man with red braces. Without thinking, the man slapped at it.

"Hyaargh," the auctioneer shouted, pointing with his hammer.

Shaun's face fell. The man with braces had outbid the Farmer. He had to do something!

Quickly, he scrambled under the canvas and snapped the arm off a sign outside that pointed the way into the auction tent.

A second later, while the auctioneer rapped his hammer – *going once* – an arm with a pointing finger appeared at the Farmer's shoulder and waggled.

Once more, the auctioneer pointed with his hammer. A last-minute bid from the man in spectacles!

The Farmer yelped. The hammer was

pointed at him!

The auctioneer looked back at the man in braces, but he shook his head. The auctioneer rapped his hammer for the final time. The Farmer was the highest bidder, and the llamas were now **SOLD!**

The auctioneer led Hector, Raul and Fernando over to the Farmer and held out his hand. It was time to pay up. The Farmer shrugged and turned his pockets out to show he had no money. He couldn't pay!

Unconvinced, the auctioneer called over a hulking helper, who rubbed his knuckles and stared menacingly at the Farmer. The Farmer shrank back.

Helpfully, Bitzer tugged at the Farmer's jacket, pointing to the inside pocket where he kept his wallet. Glaring at the sheepdog, the Farmer reluctantly took it out and handed over a thick wad of money.

As the auctioneer and his beefy assistant walked away, the Peruvian piper sidled up to Bitzer. Beaming with smiles, he hung his pipes round Bitzer's neck and ran off, laughing and clicking his heels together.

Then Bitzer spotted Shaun, who was holding a wooden arm with a pointing finger. Letting the pipes drop from his paws, Bitzer growled. It must have been Shaun who had placed the last bid for the llamas!

With a snigger, Shaun hid the wooden arm behind his back: *Whoops*!

CHAPTER THREE

AT **MOSSY BOTTOM FARM,** a group of sheep stopped munching grass and watched the horsebox trailer reverse through the gate. A cross-looking Bitzer prodded Shaun, who had been hidden behind the driver's seat, out of the vehicle.

Shaun sprinted into the meadow, bleating in excitement and proudly holding

up the broken-off pointy-finger arm he had used to bid for the llamas. The Flock wasn't going to believe what had happened! Shaun explained everything as Hazel, Nuts, the Twins, Timmy, his mum and Shirley listened breathlessly. Llamas!

Then the Flock watched as the Farmer opened the back of the trailer. In a blur and with a bray of freedom, Hector, Raul and Fernando exploded out of the horsebox and onto Mossy Bottom Farm. Ignoring the Farmer, they dashed around the farm, leaving a trail of crashes and bangs. Shouting, the Farmer gave chase. By the time he caught up, Raul was wearing a bucket on his head while Fernando and Hector played tug-of-war with an old broom.

Still shouting, the Farmer flapped his hands at the llamas. Hector snapped at his fingers.

The Farmer gulped as he looked up into three unfriendly faces. It suddenly occurred to him that the llamas were much bigger than sheep, and that their teeth were huge. With another gulp and a nervous "hmmmf", the Farmer jumped behind Bitzer and pushed him forward. Herding was the sheepdog's job. *He* could get them into the field. Without looking back, the Farmer climbed into the car and drove off towards the farmhouse.

The llamas did not like being herded. Instead, they found their way into the vegetable patch. Raul ate a pot of herbs, while Fernando found some tasty radishes.

Bitzer blew his whistle and pointed, but the llamas wouldn't listen. The sheep didn't know what to think.

Hector looked around, bored, and spotted Timmy's battered old football. With a "hmmm", he juggled it for a moment, then hoofed it towards Raul.

CLANG. The ball bounced off the bucket Raul had managed to get stuck on his head. Fernando looked up and caught the ball on the back of his neck.

"Oooooo . . ." The sheep stared at the llamas' ball skills, then looked at one another. They should play a football match! Sheep versus llamas.

With a flick of a hoof, Fernando passed the ball back towards Raul. Again, it bounced off the bucket with a clang, then flew over to Hector, who headed it neatly back to Fernando.

Bitzer wore a stern look on his face. This was not the time for games.

The llamas and the sheep took no notice of him at all. The match was on!

A second later, the ball landed at Bitzer's feet, followed by a stampede of sheep and llamas. Peeping his whistle desperately, the dog was flattened.

Meanwhile, Fernando headed the ball down the meadow with the Twins close on his hooves. Hazel was still lacing her football boots as the llama ran by. Fernando let the ball drop and dribbled it expertly. Grinning, he leapt over a sheep who was trying to tackle him and spun the ball on his hoof before whamming it towards the sheep's goal.

Hazel was still lacing her boots.

Shaun intercepted and hoofed the ball away. Fernando caught it on his head, rolled it down his back and flipped it into the air with his tail. Hector nodded it into the sheep goal. One-nil to the llamas!

For a moment, it looked like the sheep might catch up quickly. Cross-eyed with concentration, Nuts sprinted down the field with the ball rolling at his hooves. Hector grinned at him from the goal mouth. With an "ooof", Nuts slammed the ball in a perfectly aimed shot.

Hector ducked, revealing the other two llamas hidden behind him. As the ball flew, they took position –

completely blocking the goal. Sheep looked on in shock as the ball bounced off the chuckling llamas and rolled away.

Nuts wandered off, shaking his head in disappointment.

With an annoyed "whuff" Bitzer clambered to his feet again. He reached for his whistle and gave it a long, hard blow – then looked down in shock when a low, haunting sound filled the air. The sheepdog realized that he was still wearing the pipes that the llamas' previous owner had hung round his neck. He'd blown them by mistake. With a growl, he tossed them aside and blew on his whistle instead. The game was *OVER*.

Obediently, sheep trailed off towards the sheep dip for a post-match bath, passing

Hazel, who had finally finished lacing her boots. She leapt up and punched the air, then looked around at an empty meadow.

At the sound of a surprised bleat from Timmy, Shaun turned back and saw the little sheep holding up the pipes Bitzer had thrown away. He tried a few notes. The magical music of Peru drifted across the field.

Behind Timmy, the llamas' eyes instantly glazed over. The football fell from Hector's neck and rolled away. The three of them stood as still as statues.

Puzzled, Timmy lowered the pan pipes and peered at them for a second before Shaun swept him up onto his shoulders and set off towards the sheep dip. Bleating with delight, Timmy dropped the pipes into the grass. Behind him, the llamas' eyes focused. They shook their heads. Blinking, Hector stared at the set of pipes in the grass. A wicked look crossed his face. Stepping forward, he stamped.

With a **CRACK,** the pipes shattered.

Hector, Fernando and Raul looked at each other and sniggered.

CHAPTER FOUR

WHILE THE SHEEP DIP FILLED with water, Bitzer poured in a bottle of Barry Stiles' Hint of Luxury sheep shampoo and sat in his lifeguard chair, swinging his whistle and watching over the sheep. When it looked like Shaun might jump in, Bitzer half raised the whistle to his mouth and glared. With a sigh, Shaun turned and used the steps to gently lower himself into

the water, where the other sheep were sploshing around and bleating about the football match.

Bitzer blinked at the sound of galloping hooves. With a loud bray, all three llamas leapt over the wall behind him and cannonballed the pool, sending up a huge wave and soaking Bitzer.

Hector surfaced. Pursing his lips, he spat a fountain of water that hit Shaun full in the face. Shaun giggled as Raul's head bobbed out of the water. He, too, spouted a jet of water, splashing the Twins. Within seconds the two llamas were spitting water at everyone, and the rest of the sheep weren't as happy as Shaun to join in the fun. Timmy's Mum scowled when a stream from

Hector hit her, ruining the rollers she had carefully arranged on her head. She pulled Timmy away to join the angry-looking Flock at the other end of the pool.

The Flock was busy glaring at Hector and Raul and didn't notice Fernando surface behind them. Suddenly, the water round the sheep bubbled furiously. They glanced at one another. Who installed a Jacuzzi feature?

Then the smell hit them.

Fernando sighed with satisfaction: better out than in.

The bubbles had come from the llama's backside! Disgusted and gagging, sheep paddled away from the grinning llama and clambered out of the dip, grumbling and bleating and glaring at Shaun. The llamas weren't cool: they were mean, rude, selfish and smelly.

At the sound of a window opening, Bitzer looked over at the farmhouse and saw the Farmer giving him a thumbs-up and a grin. Bitzer was doing a great job! The window slammed as the Farmer disappeared back inside the house, leaving the sheepdog to deal with the llamas.

With a growl, Bitzer shot a resentful look up at the closed window and wrung water from his soaking hat.

As night fell, the Flock pushed the llamas' terrible manners out of their minds. The barn filled with the happy sounds of sheep getting ready for bed. Pillows were plumped, teeth were brushed and the sheep took it in turns to use the toilet before bedtime.

The door slammed open, letting in a cold breeze. Bleating, Shaun proudly led the llamas in and showed them the Flock's home. Hector, Fernando and Raul stared around with interest, nodding. The barn looked snug and comfy. Then they looked at one another.

At the sound of loud crashes and bangs, the sheep stopped washing and looked round.

Timmy's Mum's mouth fell open.

The three llamas had piled up all the beds into one giant, soft and comfy mound and had settled down for the night. Happily sucking his thumb, Fernando rested his head on Hector's shoulder, and closed his eyes. Snuggled up next to the llamas, Shaun was already asleep.

As llama farts drifted up into the rafters, the Flock had no choice but to squeeze into the bare hayloft. The grumpy sheep tried to find places to lie down comfortably, and instead found the sharp corners of old boxes. Shivering, they tried to sleep.

And then the snoring started.

Around the barn, eyes snapped open in alarm. Outside, several moles popped their heads out of the ground and stared at the vibrating barn in wonder, with their paws over their ears.

CHAPTER FIVE

THE MOLES WEREN'T THE ONLY ONES

kept awake by snoring llamas. When dawn arrived, a tired cockerel slumped into his usual place on the wall. With a small *merp*, he turned and limped back to the chicken run.

Inside the farmhouse, Bitzer waved his clipboard under the Farmer's nose. The sheep needed feeding, and so, too, did the

 45

llamas. It was a lot of extra work. With a grunt, the Farmer peered through the steam rising from his morning tea, nodded and stood up wearily. He'd give Bitzer a hand.

By the door, he stopped. "Oooh," he mumbled, pointing. He'd forgotten the washing-up. He was far too busy. Bitzer would have to feed the llamas on his own.

The sheepdog gave a small "whuff" – but there was only one plate to wash up!

The Farmer picked up the plate and scrubbed it busily. He glanced over at Bitzer. "Whharreyup?" he muttered.

Grumbling to himself, Bitzer gave up and went to feed the animals. Outside, he peeked back through the window. Seeing that the sheepdog was looking, the Farmer carried on pretending to wash the same plate.

Rolling his eyes, the sheepdog turned and padded over to the barn. What was the Farmer so afraid of? He put his whistle to his mouth and opened the door.

Stampeding llamas promptly trampled him. Full of energy after a good night's rest and bleating loudly, Hector, Raul and Fernando – followed by Shaun – raced into the morning sunshine, leaving a flattened Bitzer laying in the dust.

After a few moments he picked himself up, dusted himself down and peered into the barn. Inside, groaning sheep with bags under their eyes struggled out of makeshift beds, complaining loudly. They hadn't had a wink of sleep. Yawning and rubbing their eyes, they staggered outside, towards breakfast.

Bitzer warily began filling the food trough with sheep nuts. Just as the Flock stepped up to the trough, tummies growling, the sound of thundering hooves rumbled around the meadow.

Bitzer looked up. He gulped. Tossing the empty food sack over his shoulder, he ran for it.

Hector, Fernando and Raul skidded to a halt at the trough, which Hector tipped on its end. Food poured out into a pile at the llamas' feet. Instantly, they began munching their way through the entire contents of the trough. Shirley stared in horror as she watched breakfast disappear.

"Yeeeuuch!" Coughing and spluttering, the llamas lifted their heads, making

Shaun the Sheep
The
FARMER'S
LLAMAS

Bitzer and the Farmer arrive at the country fair, not noticing that Shaun has come along, too.

With their decorated sheep-cake on display, they are ready for the judges!

What's that haunting music? Fernando, Hector
and Raul are led through the fairground.

They become the latest residents of Mossy Bottom Farm!

SCORE!

The llamas are calm only when the pan pipes are played,
and they seem friendly enough, until...

The barn is ruined! The Flock aren't happy about it,
but the llamas don't care.

They move on to the farmhouse!

The Farmer and Bitzer need help!

Will Shaun find a way to save the day?

disgusted faces. Sheep food was horrible! They spat out the Flock's breakfast and scraped their tongues clean with their hooves. How could the sheep eat such rubbish? Spitting out the last few crumbs, Hector dashed to the water trough with Raul and Fernando close behind. There the llamas stopped, gazing down at the green, stagnant water in horror. A frog lay back, sunbathing.

The llamas turned their eyes towards the farmhouse, where a supermarket delivery man was unloading crates of cola. They looked back at one another, grinning and wagging their tails with glee. While they were being fed hard, tasteless sheep nuts and stagnant water, the Farmer was getting a big delivery of *proper* food and drink.

In the kitchen, the Farmer was humming happily. He had a big pile of groceries and Bitzer was dealing with the . . .

LLAMAS!

Three faces had appeared at the window, each wearing a hungry and very toothy grin. With a high-pitched "waaaah" of shock, the Farmer backed out through the kitchen door and slammed it behind himself.

Shaun's head popped up in the window too. Grinning, he looked at the goodies on the kitchen table and gave the llamas a wink.

CHAPTER SIX

PAWS ON HIS HIPS, Bitzer looked around at the mess inside the barn. He growled to himself. Someone would have to tidy it up, and – of course – it wouldn't be the Farmer. Shaking his head, he went off to fetch the vacuum cleaner.

Meanwhile, Shaun crept up the entrance hallway in the farmhouse, listening for the Farmer's footsteps. Outside, the llamas

stared through the kitchen window, watching while Shaun tip-hoofed in. Giving the llamas a thumbs up, he grabbed a bottle of cola from the crate on the kitchen table, then sneaked back out of the door, thrilled by his own daring.

The llamas looked at one another. Hector rolled his eyes. Shaun was an amateur. Hector opened the window, leaned into the kitchen and grabbed the whole crate of cola!

By the time Shaun turned the corner, holding up his swiped bottle, the llamas were each carrying bags stuffed with groceries.

Soon the four were leaning against various items of junk in the tractor shed, surrounded by half-eaten food and empty bottles. Across the meadow, the rest of the Flock looked away. Noses in the air, the tutting sheep put as much distance as they could between themselves and the thieves. Only Timmy looked interested. It was a hot day, and the cold cola called to him. Leaving the Flock behind, the little sheep trotted towards Shaun and the llamas.

Having downed half a bottle of fizzy cola in a single gulp, Fernando burped and sniggered. Hearing a tiny bleat, he looked down and saw Timmy staring at his drink longingly. Fernando handed him a bottle and tapped his own against it: *cheers!*

Overjoyed, Timmy settled himself between Shaun and Hector. He took a gulp of stolen cola and let out a tiny burp. Shaun ruffled his fleece, bleating. Life was better with a little bit of mischief. Shaun and Timmy giggled, blowing over the tops of their cola bottles to make a low and haunting noise.

Hector finished his own bottle, then threw it away, wiped his mouth and leaned back against a blue tarpaulin.

BEEP.

Raul started at the sound and lifted a corner of the tarpaulin. A wicked grin appeared on his face. Quickly, he threw the rest of the tarpaulin cover aside. Underneath was the Farmer's quad bike. Raul and Hector grinned at each other and climbed on.

BEEP, BEEPITY, BEEP-BEEP.

Shaun and Timmy looked up from their bottles and stared. The two llamas were riding the quad bike like a see-saw! Bleating with horror, Shaun jumped up and ran to stop them. This was taking mischief too far.

Behind him, Fernando finished his cola. Then he spotted Timmy's still half-full bottle, snatched it and began to guzzle, watching what Hector and Raul were up to.

Tears welled in Timmy's eyes.

At that moment, the summer day was shattered by the roar of the quad bike's engine. Shaun waved his hooves, bleating desperately. Raul and Hector had to get off. There would be big trouble if the Farmer saw them . . .

Shaun was interrupted by a wail behind him. Across the meadow, Timmy's Mum and the other sheep looked up. Timmy was crying! What had Shaun done now? As one, the Flock started running.

Shaun turned and bleated softly to Timmy, trying to comfort the sobbing lamb. But before he could even pat Timmy on the head, the quad bike hurtled past, carrying all three llamas. Shrieking with laughter, Raul leaned over, grabbed Shaun by the fleece and plonked him onto the handlebars.

BLEEEAAAAAAAAAAATTTT!

The running sheep stopped. They gawped as Shaun shot past on the front of an out-of-control quad bike. It weaved across the meadow, crashed through the gate, into the pigsty and reappeared – chasing panicked pigs across the meadow – before veering off straight towards where Timmy stood, wailing above the noise of the engine. With a terrified bleat, Timmy's Mum dashed to save him. She snatched her son into her arms just as the bike roared past and bounced away.

Raul pulled on the handlebars. The quad bike's front wheels lifted into a wheelie, and Shaun gave a sudden yelp. Up ahead, someone had left some old planks against the low stone wall. They looked, to his growing horror, very much like a ramp. A very flimsy ramp. He opened his mouth to bleat a warning. The quad bike couldn't possibly make that jump . . .

At the same time, Bitzer took a last look at his handiwork. The barn was spick and span. All the beds were made and the cushions plumped. He had dusted the furniture and hung the towels up neatly. Pleased with himself, the sheepdog shut the barn doors.

The quad bike hit the ramp. Shaun and the llamas flew through the air, holding on with all their might. For a second, Shaun's bleat could be heard above the scream of the engine. Then it was drowned out in a long series of crashes, thumps, more crashes and the squeal of metal.

The quad bike had smashed through the barn doors, ploughed through the sheep's beds, busted out again through the far wall and disappeared through the hedge.

Bitzer gawped. Behind him, the Flock gawped too. One of the quad bike's wheels rolled through the barn and toppled over at Bitzer's feet.

Clutching his head, Shaun sat up in the grass just beyond the broken hedge. He looked at the ruined barn in horror, and then bleated at the llamas. What had they done?

The llamas laughed hysterically. That was *brilliant*! Chuckling, they trotted off to look for more mischief.

Shaun followed, bleating angrily in protest.

The llamas turned back and shrugged – *whatever*. If Shaun was going to be a spoilsport, then he could get lost.

Silently, the Flock and Bitzer stared into the barn. The doors hung in bits. The bedding was torn, and the pillows were ripped to pieces. A breeze blew through a great hole in the far wall. Above, a beam creaked and dropped to the ground. The roof slumped, tiles shattering among the Flock's broken belongings.

Their home was in ruins.

Hurriedly, Bitzer herded the Flock away. The damage to the barn made it too dangerous to enter.

At that moment, the llamas rounded the corner, still chuckling. They walked by the Flock, ignoring the narrowed eyes of the sheep. Timmy's Mum bent down and picked up the pointy-finger sign that Shaun had used in the auction.

Shaun was sitting on his own by the battered barn, looking miserable. Timmy's Mum marched over to him and poked him with the giant finger. It was *all* his fault. It was his fault the llamas were here. It was his fault that Timmy had nearly been run over. It was his fault that their home had been wrecked.

Shaun bleated. He hadn't known the

llamas were going to —

Timmy's Mum interrupted him by breaking the wooden sign over his head. Dazed, he watched the Flock storm away.

The Farmer hummed "Rock Around the Crop", a catchy pop song that he had heard on the radio that morning. Clutching a bag of recycling, he pushed open the front door and walked across the yard to the recycling bin. Everything was grand. Bitzer had taken care of the llamas, the groceries were put away (though he was *sure* he had ordered more than that) and the barn was a total wreck ...

The Farmer stopped. The recycling fell to the ground. Behind thick glasses, he blinked as if doing so might change the sight before his eyes.

It didn't. Gurgling, he ran to the ruined barn, where Bitzer was sticking yellow-and-black caution tape over the doorway. The barn was a disaster site. No one could enter.

The Farmer gabbled in horror. His lovely barn! What on earth had happened?

Gently, Bitzer took him by the arm and led him away.

CHAPTER SEVEN

ALONE, SHAUN SLUMPED against the gatepost and watched the Flock. Timmy's Mum was right: it was all his fault.

Sighing and dragging his feet, he walked up to the barn and ducked under Bitzer's tape. Inside, he bent down and picked up Timmy's old teddy. Timmy would want it.

Slowly, he carried it back to the Flock. Seeing Shaun approach, the other sheep put

their front hooves on their hips and glared.

Just then, thunder rumbled and the first drops of rain began to fall. Thanks to Shaun, the Flock would have to sleep outside in a storm. Umbrellas snapped open. Turning their backs, the Flock made a wall between themselves and Shaun. The message was clear. They wanted nothing to do with him.

Shaun laid the teddy gently on the ground behind Timmy and shuffled away.

The Flock ignored him – all except Timmy. Finding his beloved teddy at his feet, the young sheep gave it a delighted cuddle and looked round. He watched Shaun shuffle over to the compost heap, where he sat unhappily in the rain.

Still groaning and jabbering about the ruined barn, the Farmer stomped back to the farmhouse with Bitzer at his side. When he found out who had wrecked it he would ...

The Farmer's voice trailed off as they passed the living-room window. Inside, the TV was blaring at full volume, showing a football match. The room was a mess. Hector was bouncing on a footstool while Fernando stood on the piano stamping on the keys to produce a horrible crash of mangled notes. Raul had his head in a lampshade.

Stiff with rage, the Farmer stared through the window. As Hector's head swung towards them, the Farmer and Bitzer dropped down.

The llamas! It must have been the llamas who wrecked the barn, and now they were wrecking the house too!

Furious, Bitzer whuffed. They had to do something. Growling, he pointed to the front door.

The Farmer ran over to the door, and, finding it locked, he threw himself against it. It wouldn't budge. His gaze fastened on the cat flap. He pointed at it, then at Bitzer.

Bitzer shrank back, shaking his head. He was no cat! The Farmer jabbered louder, stabbing his finger at the cat flap.

Bitzer finally gave a reluctant nod. Humiliated, the sheepdog squeezed himself through the flap.

Still beside himself with rage, the Farmer dropped to his knees to follow Bitzer, but

the cat flap swung back, right into the Farmer's face.

Bitzer paused. A frown crossed his face as he looked back at the Farmer, smashed in the face by the door. Something was wrong – or perhaps familiar? – with this situation, but he couldn't quite put his paw on it.

The farmer crawled through, and the two of them crept down the hallway, each grabbing a weapon along the way; though Bitzer was certain that a rubber spatula and a tennis racket probably wouldn't be very effective.

The Farmer shushed Bitzer and readied his spatula. Brays of excitement mingled with the sounds of a football match in the lounge. The llamas were distracted. Step by creeping step, the Farmer tiptoed in.

And stepped on the remote.

The picture on the television screen changed: instead of a decisive goal being scored, a jolly children's TV presenter was singing "The Wheels on the Bus".

The llamas, with outraged fury in their eyes, turned towards the intruders who had dared to change the channel.

The broken pointy-finger sign across his knees, Shaun glanced towards the Flock. They still had their backs turned to him.

He heard a crash and the tinkle of breaking glass from the direction of the farmhouse. The crash was followed by the muffled sound of the Farmer yelling in fear. Shaun was on his hooves instantly, dashing towards the house.

Only Timmy saw him go.

Moments later, Shaun peered through the cat flap to the hallway beyond, where the Farmer and Bitzer scrambled to escape the charging llamas. The Farmer disappeared up the stairs with Raul close behind him. Loud thumps and bumps came from the floor above when the Farmer threw himself into a wardrobe and slammed the doors behind him.

With a small click, the latch fell into place, locking him in.

Meanwhile, Fernando stalked silently through the kitchen, his head swinging this way and that, his nostrils flaring. Bitzer was hiding somewhere . . . but where?

The llama started checking the kitchen cabinets, and he didn't get far before he

found Bitzer. Squashed into a cabinet like a contortionist, the dog coughed and gave Fernando an embarrassed wave.

Two seconds later, Bitzer flew out of the front door with a llama hoof printed on his backside.

Shaun, relieved to find his friend alive, ran over to Bitzer and pulled him into a hug. Holding out a hoof, he bleated an apology. He was sorry about the llamas. Would Bitzer help him get rid of them?

Staggering to his feet, Bitzer folded his arms and tapped a foot. *It was all very well bleating "sorry" but . . .*

Shaking his head, Shaun interrupted. He *really* was sorry.

Suddenly, they heard the sounds of more breaking glass inside the house and the llamas' laughter. Bitzer covered his mouth in fright. The Farmer was still in danger!

Shaun bleated and held up a hoof. He had a plan.

CHAPTER EIGHT

INSIDE THE WARDROBE, the Farmer shouted and banged on the walls of his tiny prison. It rocked from side to side as he threw himself against the wooden panels.

With a sudden splintering, the bottom gave way and the wardrobe rose up, revealing the Farmer's feet. He realized he could now shuffle around the room while still inside the wardrobe.

"Ah-haa-ooooer," he said in a muffled voice.

The wardrobe immediately crashed into the bed, then a chest of drawers.

Dusk was falling upon Mossy Bottom Farm. Inside the farmhouse, the TV blared. Surrounded by litter, food wrappers and empty bottles, Hector, Raul and Fernando were sprawled over the lounge sofa, howling at the footballers onscreen. The llamas were too busy watching the game to notice Shaun and Bitzer outside the window, pulling at the end of a rope.

The sheep and sheepdog heaved. On the roof, the satellite dish shifted.

The llamas blinked at the TV as the picture went fuzzy. Then it cleared.

Shaun and Bitzer pulled at the rope again. This time, the satellite dish came away with a crunch and crashed into a flower bed.

The TV screen turned to static as, outside the window, Shaun dashed away carrying the dish.

The llamas screamed. What had happened to the football match? The window banged open and Hector's head appeared, peering into the farmyard. He spotted the broken satellite dish in the corner of the yard.

The llamas stalked out of the front door, scowling. When they found out who had broken the TV, they would . . .

As one, they turned at the sound of a squeaky wheel.

At that moment, Shaun and Bitzer jumped out from their hiding place. Bitzer shook his bottom at the llamas. Then both he and Shaun made faces before dashing away.

Hector, Raul and Fernando stared. Their jaws dropped open. Hector gave a strangled bleat. Nobody, but nobody, made fun of llamas – especially little sheep and weird dogs.

Braying angrily, they charged round the corner – and slipped on a trail of shaving foam Bitzer had sprayed onto the ground. Unable to control their sliding hooves, the three llamas hurtled into the back of the open horsebox trailer.

They hit their heads on the far end, then turned, dazed, to see Shaun calmly press the button to lower the metal door and trap them inside.

It had worked! Shaun and Bitzer high-fived each other.

But their problems weren't over yet. Shaun and Bitzer looked up in horror as a wardrobe suddenly burst through the upstairs bedroom window, see-sawing precariously on the ledge. They heard muffled shouts – the Farmer was inside!

Bitzer woofed in alarm. With Shaun close behind, he leapt for the farmhouse door, then pounded up the stairs and into the bedroom. Bitzer saw the Farmer's feet sticking out of the wardrobe, so he grabbed both of them and pulled. Shaun tried to pull on the wardrobe itself.

But with the Farmer inside, it was too heavy. Creaking under the strain, the wardrobe slowly tipped out of the window. Wood splintered as the Farmer slid forward, his head breaking through the top panel. With a sharp crack, more wood snapped, and the top panel broke away. Screaming, scrabbling at the air and wearing the top panel like a wooden ruff, the Farmer fell towards the ground below with Bitzer desperately clinging to his ankles.

"Aaaaaarrrrrggggh . . . Ooof!"

Hearing all the commotion, the Flock had come to the rescue! Shirley, the biggest sheep, had been pushed to exactly the right spot. The Farmer bounced off her soft fleece and landed on his feet. Bitzer, too, bounced to safety.

The wardrobe hit Shirley and sprang off.

The Farmer blinked, bewildered to be standing in the farmyard, and chuckled to himself. He wasn't quite sure how it had happened, but he was safe and, even better, he wasn't trapped in a wardrobe!

Then the wardrobe fell neatly over his head.

"Bah," yelled the Farmer, hammering on the inside of the door with his fists.

SLAM!

The sheep looked round, startled by the noise. Timmy's Mum gave a frightened bleat, pointing with a hoof. The trailer's door was open.

The llamas had escaped!

But Shaun couldn't see the trailer from the upstairs window. The Flock waved frantically at him, jumping up and down.

He waved back. The Flock must be happy that the llamas were trapped and everyone was safe, he told himself.

Sheep bleated loudly, flapping their hooves in warning. The llamas were free!

Behind Shaun, a floorboard creaked. He turned round slowly.

Hector was standing in the doorway. And he did not look happy.

In fact, Shaun decided, he looked about as unhappy as a llama could possibly look. Hector glared at Shaun.

Shaun blinked back.

Then the llama took a menacing step forward. Shaun ducked to one side, then dived under the bed and slid across the floor as Hector tried to follow. He scrabbled

 79

out the other side and dashed for the door—but instead ran straight into Raul, who made a grab for him. Dodging, Shaun leap-frogged over his back and onto the landing. Fernando was waiting by the stairs.

He was trapped!

Then Shaun spotted a cord hanging from the ceiling. He jumped, caught it and tugged with all his strength. Above, a hatch fell open and a set of steps telescoped out, pinning Fernando's head to the floor: *the ladder into the attic!*

Shaun scampered up at top speed.

At the top, he breathed a sigh of relief. He was safe. Llamas couldn't climb. Could they?

Metal clanked behind him: hooves on the ladder's rungs. Hector's head slowly

rose through the hatch like a periscope, surveying the dim attic.

Shaun held his breath as he hid behind an old box of junk, pressing his back against it. He slid to the side, further into the corner.

HOOONK!

A horrible, out-of-tune squealing sound filled the attic. Shaun had pushed against a set of old bagpipes that the Farmer had inherited from a Scottish ancestor.

Hector's head swung round towards the sound, just in time to see Shaun scramble through a skylight onto the roof.

Gulping, Shaun crawled along the ridge at the top of the farmhouse. He felt dizzy from the height. From up here he could see all the way to Mossy Bottom Village, and in the distance was the glow of the big city.

Behind him came a grinding, crashing noise. Hector had forced his head through the roof, knocking off some tiles! The other two llamas quickly followed his example.

Trembling, Shaun edged backwards as the llamas dragged the rest of their bodies through the tiles, leaving gaping holes in the roof. Shaun was reminded that llamas had very, *very* big teeth. The three menacing llamas stalked towards him, dislodged tiles skittering to the edge of the roof and tumbling down below.

Meanwhile, Bitzer and the frightened Flock craned their necks, trying to see what was happening above. A roof tile crashed to the ground, nearly hitting Bitzer, and he backed into the Farmer's forgotten recycling. Empty bottles rolled across the farmyard.

Timmy picked one up and bleated quietly. When no one listened, he held up the bottle and bleated again – loudly.

Up on the roof, Shaun backed against the chimney.

The llamas were getting closer.

With nowhere else to go, Shaun scrambled up until he perched on top of the chimney pot. He bleated in fright. Behind him was only empty space and a very long fall. Clenching his teeth, Shaun squeezed his eyes closed, waiting for the end.

Hearing a strangely familiar sound, Shaun opened his eyes again. He looked over his shoulder.

It was only Timmy, standing behind him and blowing over the top of a cola bottle.

Shaun blinked, and looked over his shoulder again. How was Timmy standing on air?

The llamas were also confused by the sight. For a moment, they stopped and stared. The sound from the bottle was a little like the sound of pan pipes, but Timmy could play only one note. Snickering, they brayed: it wasn't enough. Nice try, but too bad, kid!

A different note sounded, soft and windy like Peruvian pipes, then another and another. The notes turned into a tune, as more sheep joined in. Not quite believing what he was seeing, Shaun looked down. Timmy was standing on his mum's shoulders. She, too, was playing a cola bottle, and below her were Hazel and the Twins, all blowing over the tops of their own bottles. Below *them* was a pyramid of sheep, all standing on the platform the Farmer used to pick fruit from the highest branches of the apple trees. Every sheep was blowing on a bottle. An eerie, enchanting tune rolled across the fields of Mossy Bottom Farm.

Shaun looked back at the llamas. Raul's and Fernando's eyes had glazed over already. Hector fought the music for a little longer. His lip curled in a snarl that seemed to say, "Dratted sheep"; then he, too, was mesmerized by the haunting tune. Together, the three hypnotized llamas slid down the roof and fell into the trailer below.

 85

A tear pricking the corner of his eye, Shaun gazed down at his friends in gratitude. On the ground below, Nuts waved up at him from the controls of the tractor. He pulled a lever and the platform moved a little closer to the roof. With a sigh of relief, Shaun stepped onto it.

By the time he reached the ground, the spell of the haunting music was wearing off. Inside the trailer, Hector shook his head. When he looked up, he saw Shaun press the button to close the mechanical door once again; this time, he was also holding a large padlock.

Exhausted, the llamas didn't even try to escape. They were locked in and set to leave Mossy Bottom Farm at last.

CHAPTER NINE

THE LLAMAS SHOOK their heads as the music stopped. When the hypnotism cleared, they looked round in horror at a familiar scene. Behind them was a wig-wearing man holding a hammer. In front of them was a crowd of people.

The auctioneer peered into the crowd with a shrug. Did no one want to buy the llamas?

In the distance, a man laughed.

Peering through the crowd, Shaun spotted the same man who had laughed when the Farmer bought the llamas. A mischievous grin appeared on Shaun's face. He nudged Bitzer.

A few seconds later, the auctioneer heard a whistle. At the back of the crowd he spotted a chuckling man wearing braces. He was waving an arm, its finger pointing to the ceiling.

The auctioneer rapped with his gavel:
SOLD!

The man looked around, chuckling, to see which idiot had bought the llamas this time. All he saw was a huge man forcing his way towards him through the crowd. The huge man stopped and loomed over the smirking man with braces, who then spluttered and turned red, realizing what was happening. The auctioneer's payment collectors ignored his protests, and eventually the man reluctantly dipped into a pocket for his wallet. The payment collector handed him three ropes and left him with Hector, Fernando, and Raul, who immediately tried to make a break for it.

With a growl, the man with braces tugged them back.

The llamas blinked.

Their new owner glared at them. This time, they had met their match. Grumbling, he dragged them away.

Just behind where the man had stood, Bitzer waved the pointy-finger sign with a grin. The three llamas had been paid for.

Hector, Raul and Fernando were someone else's problem now!

Chuckling happily, the Farmer walked over and took the sign off him, waving it in celebration.

At the podium, the auctioneer's hammer cracked onto wood again. Shaun looked up and saw the beefy collector already making his way towards the Farmer.

Then he looked towards the holding pen.

A huge, grey head with beady eyes and a horn glared at him. A deep roar drowned out every sound in the tent.

Shaun grinned. He'd always wanted a rhinoceros as a friend.

Check out these books
for more

SHEEP
SHENANIGANS!

Also available as eBooks

THE FLOCK FACTOR

It's talent-show time at Mossy Bottom Farm! Shaun discovers that Shirley could be a big star, but will she get over her stage fright and perform in front of the judges?

THE BEAST OF SOGGY MOOR

What's that howling sound? What's that looming figure? The animals are in a panic: a terrible beast is on the prowl! It's up to Shaun and Bitzer to set a trap and save the farm.

ON THE BALL

The sheep have invented a great new game, and the pigs challenge them to a match. But when the pigs keep changing the rules, how will the Flock even the score?

FLOCK TO THE SEASIDE

Bitzer faces the biggest challenge of his career as a sheepdog: the Piddlington-on-Sea Annual Sheepdog Trial. The trouble is, the Flock is more interested in the nearby beach… Oops!

PRANKS A LOT!

When Shaun the Sheep plays a practical joke on Bitzer, the sheepdog has to get revenge. But as one prank leads to another, the tricks get out of hand. Who will get the last laugh?

BLAST TO THE PAST

After their go-kart crashes, Shaun and the Flock find that the farm has changed. The tractor looks new, the pigs are wearing diapers, and the Farmer has an earring! Have they gone back in time?